Bear & Katie
in
A Day at Nestlenook Farm

By Loni R. Burchett

Illustrated by Patricia Sweet-MacDonald

Other books by Loni Burchett

Bear and Katie in The Great Searsport Caper

Released 2004

Written by Loni R. Burchett
Illustrated by Patricia Sweet-MacDonald
Edited by Nancy Grossman and Kay Harrison

Published by
Black Lab Publishing, LLC
P.O. Box 64
Alton, NH 03809
blacklabpub@hotmail.com
www.bearandkatie.com

Printed by Morgan Press, Manchester, NH
Published and manufactured in the U.S.A.

First Printing: November, 2004

ISBN: 0-9742815-1-4

Dedicated to

My Uncle and Aunt, Woody and Doris Waggoner, whom I loved dearly.

Amherst, an 11-year-old Boxer better known as Ammy.

And to Bear and Katie forever: Who truly live up to the old saying; "A dog is a man's best friend."

Special Thanks to the following people:

David Edwards, advisor and life long friend. For always being there for me as a true friend would.

Richard Haynes, free lance photographer, artist and friend. For all the countless hours he spent helping me to achieve my goals.

Nancy Grossman, artist, writer, editor and wonderful friend. For her inspiration and encouragement.

Pauline Burchett, for reading every "Bear and Katie" story.

Acknowledgements:

Luxury Mountain Getaways
Route 16
Jackson, New Hampshire

The Nestlenook Farm Resort
Jackson Village, New Hampshire

Preface

I wrote the Bear and Katie stories so children could learn about the environment, our precious wild-life, geographical locations and family values, all while having fun with Bear and Katie. Through these stories, young readers will travel to exciting places and join in adventures with these two fun-loving black labs.

These two unique labs could be anyone's dogs. Become friends with Bear and Katie and tag along on their adventures everywhere our two friends travel!

Note: Bear wears a red collar. Katie prefers to wear a blue scarf.

Bear and Katie always refer to their owners as Dad and Mom.

Table of Contents

Introduction: Christmas in New England

There is nothing like a New England Christmas. From Connecticut to Maine, from Vermont to Massachusetts and from New Hampshire to Rhode Island, the six states make up what we all call New England which has its own special traditions.

Country roads lined by stonewalls and blanketed with snow, glistening on the trees. Small villages nestled in the hillsides and mountains, small in population but large in spirit. Cozy Country Inns, brilliantly decorated; offering sleigh rides in the snow.

Churches with tall steeples, lit by candle light as church bells toll, can be seen from afar. A beautiful Christmas tree stands in the middle of a gazebo in the center of a park decorated by the town residents for everyone to enjoy, as they listen to carolers singing *Silent Night*.

Strolling along the streets shoppers enjoy old fashioned stores with New England made gifts, traditional homemade candy and a sample of hot apple cider, while looking for that special gift.

A ride in the country is always a treat; snow covered bridges draped with Christmas lights and wreaths, and children skating under a bridge, a common sight to see in New England.

Along the seacoast, lighthouses dominate the coastline with beautiful decorations and lights that can be seen by boats out at sea.

New Englanders are proud of their traditions and really know how to bring the spirit of Christmas to their towns and enjoy the holiday the old fashioned way.

Bear and Katie know quite well how to enjoy the holiday, as they take you with them to Nestlenook Farm.

A Day at Nestlenook Farm

It's the Christmas Season again and like everyone else, it's Bear and Katie's favorite time of the year. All across America families are preparing for the holiday. From California to New Jersey, families decorate their trees in their own unique way.

In the southwest families are filling piñatas full of candy and toys, a tradition carried on for many generations. In the mid-west families are gathering around their fireplaces, enjoying a cup of eggnog, while loved ones share Christmas stories. In the south, kinfolk gather at grandma's house for an old fashioned feast.

But, in New England... families gather at their favorite skating ponds. Children go sledding and enjoy traditional sleigh rides.

It's a time for giving and receiving gifts, playing in the snow and making snowmen. But what Bear and Katie love the most is a trip to Nestlenook Farm. Across the Jackson covered bridge in New Hampshire sits the small Victorian village tucked away in the White Mountains. The beautiful village attracts thousands of visitors. Some folks call it a winter wonderland with a Currier and Ives atmosphere. There they'll skate on Emerald Lake, have fun mingling with hundreds of people and other dogs, sledding and going on sleigh rides.

It's early in the morning. Bear wakes and rises slowly to her feet. She does a little shake that looks more like a twist. As she walks to the window, she takes a look at her friend Katie lying on the floor on her side. She shakes her head and smiles. "Katie, you lazy old hound," she whispers and chuckles a little dog laugh.

Bear takes a big yawn, looks out the window and back to Katie when she suddenly sees Katie roll onto her other side.

"Katie!" she barks. "It's snowing outside, Katie! Wake up! It's just beautiful outside! You have to see this!"

Katie rolls over again and lets out a soft sleepy whine.

Katie hates to be woken up. "Oh for dog's sake! Why can't a dog get some sleep around here?" she growls.

Katie yawns wide and rubs her eyes with her paws, she yawns wide again and rubs her eyes again. Katie is still lying on the floor trying to wake up, when she realizes what Bear is telling her.

Snowing! Katie thinks to herself. Still half asleep, she opens one eye.

"Snowing. It's snowing!" she barks.

Katie jumps to her feet, stretches her front legs out, and bends down for a big morning stretch. Then she stands up to shake herself off. Still sleepy, she stumbles over to where Bear is standing and gazes out the window.

"You're right, Bear! It's snowing, and it is just beautiful. Today is the day we go to Nestlenook Farm for a sleigh ride. Oh, boy! I can't wait!"

"I'm so glad it's snowing," says Bear, "especially since it's the day before Christmas."

"Oh yes," replies Katie. "It will make the sleigh ride more exciting. Snow falling on our noses! It will be like a winter wonderland," she barks.

"I'm anxious to help build a snowman," says Bear, wagging her tail. She has visions in her head of Katie and her building a giant snowman.

"You're really good at supervising," laughs Katie, picturing Bear just sitting and watching everyone work—something Bear does very well.

Bear grumbles at Katie. "Well, at least I'm good at being creative. I tell everyone where to put the snowballs. You, on the other hand, spend more time chasing the snowballs. You think you're a snowball retriever," Bear chuckles with a loud bark.

"This time, I will be more careful," says Katie. "I'll let them roll the snowballs into large ones for the snowman, instead of retrieving them. It's going to be fun! Lots of fun!" she laughs.

Bear and Katie rush to eat breakfast. They are so anxious to get on the road they gobble up their food and then run to grab their leashes and dog mittens.

Dad and Mom finish their breakfast. "I want to find a tree farm on our way home today," says Mom. "This is the first time that we have waited so long at Christmas to put up a tree."

"Yes, you're right, but I promise you, we will get the prettiest one in the forest. Maybe Bear and Katie will help us find it," Dad tells her.

Bear and Katie rush outside and wait for Mom and Dad, who are still looking for their skates.

"Well, we can't find our skates, so we will just have to rent a pair when we get there. So... are you two ready?" asks Dad. Bear and Katie both give him three loud barks. "Yes! Yes! Yes!"

"Are you going to go sledding?" asks Bear, remembering how Katie took a big plunge in a snowbank the year before and rolled down the hill, until she looked like a giant dog snowman.

Katie looks at Bear with a grin. "You bet I am! But I think I will try to stay on the sled this time. The snow can get quite cold when you roll in it, all the way down the hill, that is!" She laughs out a bark.

"Bear, do you remember the time Dad and Mom went skiing over in Vermont?"

"Oh yes," chuckles Bear. "It was in March when the resorts offer a day of free ski lessons and Mom thought she could learn to be a great skier."

"Yes," replies Katie, "The ski instructor had a group on the hillside and asked Mom to join them. She said she knew what she was doing and began to ski down the hill," Katie continues.

"She thought she was doing really well, but when she picked up speed, she tried to slow down and one of her skis crossed over the other one. Mom took a big dive—face first into the snow. Right in front of a crowd of people," Katie laughs.

"That must have been a really embarrassing moment," chuckles Bear.

"Oh! And remember the time Dad got tickets to go skiing in Idaho?" asks Katie. "Poor Dad waited all year for that trip and when they rode up the slope, the chair lift stopped," she continues.

"And it took hours to get it running again. Dad just laughed, but Mom, being the scaredy cat that she is, never went on a chair lift again," says Bear with a slow whine, and a big grin. "Then there was the time in New York City. Mom shopped all day and took us all over the city and to Central Park."

"Oh yes," says Katie with a smile. "There's nothing more beautiful than New York City* during the holiday. Oh... the lights! The beautiful lights."

Bear and Katie are having so much fun reminiscing.

Bear looks out the window of the truck when Dad begins to sing. "Oh the weather outside is frightful."

Then Mom begins to sing. "But the snow is so delightful."

Then Bear and Katie join in, "So let it snow, let it snow, let it snow!" The two dogs laugh, sing and howl all the way down the road.

---

*See, *Bear & Katie See the Big Apple*

A few hours later they cross the Jackson covered bridge and arrive at the Nestlenook Farm. Bear and Katie jump to their feet and begin to wag their tails. They wait patiently for Dad to let them out of the truck.

"There must be a hundred or more people here," woofs Bear.

"Look at all the skaters standing in line to rent skates," says Dad, as he turns to look at Mom. "I hope there will be some left over for us," he continues.

"I guess I better hurry and get in line, before they are all gone," she replies.

"I'll stay here with Bear and Katie," Dad tells her.

Bear and Katie are not paying attention to Dad and Mom's conversation. They are so excited about being at Nestlenook Farm.

"Oh boy! What should we do first?" asks Bear.

"Let's ask Dad!" cries Katie.

The two labs turn and look at Dad.

"Well girls, what do you want to do?" asks Dad, while Mom makes her way over to the skate rental shed to take her place in line.

Bear and Katie look at each other with serious looks on their faces. They both rub their chins with their paws and begin to look around.

"Gee! There is so much to do here," woofs Katie.

"Let's go sledding first," suggests Bear.

Katie is so excited she doesn't object to anything. She is ready to have some fun! "Sounds good to me," barks Katie.

They spot a large crowd of children who are gathered at the top of a hill. Bear and Katie take off running, flinging snow everywhere with their paws. Quickly their run turns into a full gallop, all the way to the top.

Two boys are about to climb on a sled. Bear asks if she can have a ride, but Katie has no time to wait and jumps on the back of a toboggan sled already going down the hill.

Bear is embarrassed. She looks at the two boys, and shakes her head.

"You just have to excuse my friend," she exclaims. "She gets so excited she doesn't stop to think about manners."

The two boys just laugh. "That's okay! We understand."

"You must be Bear and Katie?" asks one of the boys.

"Why, yes!" answers Bear curiously. "How did you know we're Bear and Katie?"

"Everyone here at Nestlenook Farm talks about the two black labs who come here every year. Bear is known for being well-mannered. That must be you? And Katie is known as the fun-loving dog that gets into mischief. So when we first saw you two running up the hill, we figured it must be Bear and Katie," says the boy, with a smile on his face.

"So jump on, Bear! Let's go for a ride."

Bear is having so much fun running up the hill and sliding back down, waving her paw at Katie as she passes by her. Katie is her usual self, falling and rolling down the hill.

Just as they pass a crowd of people building a snowman, Bear jumps off the sled. She is sure they need her help. Katie takes a quick dive into the snow and shakes herself off. She runs to meet up with Bear.

Bear and Katie begin to roll snowballs with their noses, pushing the snowballs as hard as they can, until they are too large for them to push. The crowd of children cheers their black lab friends as they build a big beautiful snowman.

"Hey! Let's build two more snowmen and put dog-ears and tails on them and we can call them Bear and Katie," one of the boys suggests. The two labs love the idea and chuckle a few soft barks, their bark of approval.

Boys and girls join in together to build the dog snowmen. Bear and Katie push again with their noses, until the snowballs are too big for them to push.

A boy tells Katie to help him roll another giant snowball, for the finishing touches. Katie begins to push the snow until it forms a nice big snowball. Bear and Katie are thrilled that the snow dogs are beginning to look like them.

The dog-ears and tails are placed on the dog snowmen carefully. Then they all step back and look.

"I think they look great," says Katie.

"I think they look just... like us," laughs Bear. Everyone is pleased. Bear and Katie get a pat on the head and hugs.

The children are enjoying Bear and Katie's company, and Bear and Katie are enjoying the children's company.

"How about another ride down the hill?" barks Katie.

"You can ride with me," suggests one of the boys. "Oh! By the way, my name is Erik."

"Katie, you can ride on the saucers with me" says Erik. "And... Bear can ride with my friend Ryan."

"We can go to the tip-top of the hill and take a real long ride down," says Ryan, with his sled tucked under his arm.

Bear and Katie turn to look at each other, and with a loud bark, they take off up the hill.

Erik and Ryan run right behind them. The four of them ride down the hill and run back up again.

The other children cheer as the two labs pass them. Bear and Katie chuckle out a little bark as they pass by the dog snowmen.

"Well! Now that we've helped build the snowmen or should we say, snow dogs," laughs Katie, "what should we do, Bear?"

Bear and Katie begin to walk towards the pond.

"Katie! Look at all the skaters on the lake. Oh! I wish I could skate." Bear tells her with a loud bark.

"I may not be a skater, but I sure am going to try today," replies Katie with a cautious look on her funny lab face.

Bear just grins, she knows Katie will try to skate if it's the last thing she does. "Katie, I have never seen a dog skate. Although I would love to see it, I really don't think it can be done," ruffs Bear.

"Well, this may be your lucky day!" replies Katie. "I just might give it a try. That's if my paws don't get too cold." She continues with a woof.

"That's what our dog mittens are for," answers Bear. "But you never wear them."

Bear takes a look around and spots Dad and Mom skating on the pond.

"Oh look! There's Dad and Mom skating," barks Bear.

"Let's go join them!" answers Katie, with a soft whine.

Bear shakes the snow off her paws and nose, while Katie takes off running.

"Slow down, Katie!" shouts Bear. "You're going to fall into the skaters."

"Don't worry, Bear. I know what I'm doing!" Katie shouts with a loud bark as she heads for the pond.

Bear knows Katie is reckless, and covers her eyes with both paws.

Suddenly, Katie hits the ice. She skids all the way across the pond on three paws, with her fourth one in the air. She lands in a snowbank close to a group of children sitting on a bench putting on their skates. Everyone begins to laugh, as they look at Katie with only her tail and back legs sticking out of the snowbank.

"What a sight to see!" laughs a little girl. "Look at that funny black dog, all covered in snow. She's a white dog now, ha ha!"

Katie wiggles her way out of the snowbank as Bear helps dig the snow away from her face.

"Katie, you never learn! What would you do without me?" laughs Bear.

"I don't know, but I sure am glad to have you here with me," chuckles Katie, with an embarrassed look on her snow-covered face.

"How about we go over to the campfire and rest," suggests Dad.

"I think we could use a rest too," Bear says to Katie. "I bet they are going to have hot cocoa with marshmallows. Yummy!"

"I wish we could have some, but we'll have to settle for water," says Katie.

Bear and Katie see Dad reaching into his pocket. "Let's follow Dad and Mom to the campfire, Dad has chewies in his pocket for us," barks Bear, who always has time to break for a chewy.

Just as Dad and Mom sit down, Katie suddenly turns and heads in another direction.

"Where are you going, Katie?" asks Bear.

Katie, looking toward the trees, turns to Bear. "Shh... I see a rabbit," she answers. "I'll be right back."

"Don't be running off, for Pete's sake. You'll get lost," cries Bear.

As usual, Katie doesn't listen and runs right into the woods following the rabbit's tracks in the snow. She suddenly hears a loud crashing sound. When she looks she sees a boulder heading toward her. Before the boulder reaches her, Katie feels a strong thump to her hip and is knocked out of the way of the large rock. Katie falls into the snow. When she gets up on her feet, she shakes the snow off and begins to look around to see what might have bumped her to knock her out of the way.

Puzzled, Katie shakes herself off again. Forgetting about the rabbit, she quickly runs back to find Bear.

"Bear! Bear! You wouldn't believe what happened to me. Or... maybe you already know?" she barks, all excited.

"What are you talking about, Katie? What do you mean by, I might already know?" Bear grumbles to Katie.

"You mean you weren't in the woods and knocked me out of the way of a falling boulder?" she asks Bear.

"No Katie, I've been here all the time you were gone," says Bear, still grumbling. She is not sure what to think about Katie's little adventure in the woods.

Katie seems puzzled. "Well, I wonder what knocked me out of the way of that boulder that almost hit me," she tells Bear, mumbling as they turn to walk toward the campfire where Dad and Mom are sitting. "You know, I could use that rest after all," Katie continues.

"And enjoy the chewy Dad was taking out of his pocket before you went running off after a rabbit," whines Bear.

"Yeah! And let's hurry before they take the sleigh ride without us," replies Katie.

The two black labs make their way back to where Dad and Mom are sitting, enjoying a cup of hot chocolate.

Dad takes a few chewies out of his pocket for his wonderful fun-loving dogs.

"Yum! Yum! It's chewy time!" barks Bear. The two enjoy their treat.

Bear and Katie lie down for a brief rest.

"Well, Bear and Katie, are you girls having a good time?" asks Dad as he gives his happy labs another treat.

Bear and Katie spot the sleigh coming. They drop their chewies and jump to their feet, bark three times and pick their chewies up again.

"I guess that's a Yes!" laughs Dad.

Bear and Katie look toward the horses and sleigh, anxious to take a ride.

Dad rubs Bear on the head and Mom hugs Katie. They are happy to see Bear and Katie having such a good time.

"Yes, girls, we will be going there next. We have to get these skates off and then we'll go for a sleigh ride."

Bear and Katie roll over and over in the snow to show how happy they are. Then they shake themselves off. Dad and Mom cover their faces as the two labs fling snow all over them.

Dad and Mom take off their skates and finish their hot chocolate.

The Sleigh Ride and
Bear Senses Danger

"Well, now let's go on a sleigh ride, Bear and Katie!" suggests Dad.

Bear and Katie take off running as fast as they can. They are way ahead of Dad and Mom, and already standing in line waiting as they arrive at the sleigh.

Dad helps his two pooches on the sleigh and off they go. Bear and Katie love it when the sleigh goes into the woods. They watch eagerly to spot a deer, rabbit or even a moose. Katie has her head on Mom's lap and Bear is sitting alert, looking all around.

Everyone begins to sing Christmas carols. Bear and Katie are happy to finally get on the sleigh. This is their favorite treat at the Nestlenook Farm. People come from everywhere to take a ride on their fine sleighs.

As they approach a curve on the trail, Bear becomes restless. Her ears perk up and she suddenly leaps off the sleigh, running far ahead of it. She begins to cross the road, sniffing, until she is no longer in sight.

Katie is shocked! "This isn't like Bear at all!" she's thinking. Dad becomes very nervous, as he begins to wonder what could have caused Bear to react in such a way. He looks at Katie for an answer.

"What do you think is going on?" Dad asks Katie. "I would expect this from you, but not from Bear," he says, very confused and worried. Then he continues, "Not to imply that you aren't a good dog, but you are always very curious... and get into a few fixes," Dad says, as he reassures Katie he loves her too, rubbing her behind the ears.

"I'm not sure," barks Katie. "It must be very important. Bear must sense something's wrong. You know how well Bear can sense danger," continues Katie, with a few soft whines. She jumps off the sleigh to go join her best friend.

"Bear! Wait for me!" Katie shouts, with a loud bark.

Katie runs to catch up with Bear, who is already out of sight of the sleigh and around the bend.

"Bear!" shouts Katie. "Where are you? Is something wrong?"

"Over here Katie, I'm over here!" she yips.

Katie follows Bear's yip and finally catches up with her.

Bear turns and looks at Katie.

"Look Katie! Look what I found," she says with a soft whisper. "It's a baby deer, and it looks like her leg is caught under that fallen tree," Bear says. "I heard a faint cry and came here to see what was wrong," continued Bear.

"Oh yes! I'm glad I came to help out," says Katie.

"I am worried about the tree banch on the little deer's leg," whines Bear.

"Yes, and the tree is too close to the road, and when the sleigh comes around the next bend, it may frighten everyone, even the fawn," Katie says with a scared look on her face.

"Help me! Help me!" cries the small deer.

"What should we do?" Katie asks nervously.

"Well, I need you to run back to the sleigh to warn the driver that there is danger here. While you are gone, I'll begin to dig around the bottom of this huge tree branch, near the fawn's leg, and see if I can free her. Now hurry!"

Katie takes off running. Running so fast, she is out of breath when she reaches the sleigh. She can hardly bark. She takes a moment to catch her breath. Then she begins to bark aggressively.

Dad knows instantly that there is something seriously wrong. "Stop the sleigh," he shouts to the driver. "Stop the sleigh!"

The driver stops the sleigh and then jumps off. Dad jumps off right behind him.

Everyone on the sleigh is silent, waiting to see what all the excitement is about.

Katie is panting and out of breath.

"Where is your friend?" shouts the driver.

"Where is Bear?" asks Dad.

Dad pauses, then pats Katie on the head. "What is wrong, girl?"

She looks at Dad with a frightened expression on her face. "It's Bear! She needs our help," Katie barks softly.

"Katie, take us to Bear," he whispers. Dad doesn't want to frighten the others on the sleigh. Dad asks the sleigh driver to assist him and they begin to follow Katie up the trail.

When they get to where Bear and the small fawn are, they see Bear digging frantically. The driver and Dad grab one end of the huge tree branch with their hands and begin to try to lift it.

Bear and Katie are both digging now. The small deer looks at Bear and Katie with a frightened sigh.

"By the way, I'm really glad to see you two come to my rescue. My mother was in the woods when I ran off. She must be looking for me. But now this huge tree branch has fallen on me," the fawn snorts. "Maybe I can find her, if I can get out of this awful mess," she says with a sigh.

"By the way, you can call me Dottie. I'm a fawn. That's what they call us small deer. FAWNS," she says with pride, as she grunts trying to free her leg from under the tree.

"Well, we are happy to meet you and even happier to be here to help you," Bear ruffs.

"We are Bear and Katie! At your service, I might add!" Katie tells her new little friend Dottie. "Please don't try to free your leg. It might make things worse. Let us do it for you," she says with a soft woof.

But Dottie is scared and in a lot of pain, as everyone tries to free her from the fallen tree branch.

"This is Dad and the sleigh driver," Bear tells her. "They have come to help free you. It shouldn't take long now."

"I think my leg might be broken," she cries, with a slight snort. "It really hurts."

"We'll have to take her directly to the Nestlenook Farm caretaker as soon as we get this tree branch off of her leg," Dad tells Bear and Katie.

Bear and Katie keep digging and Dad and the sleigh driver keep tugging and pulling on the large tree branch.

Bear and Katie hear a sound coming from the woods. When they turn to look, they see another deer. "Are you Dottie's mother?" Bear ruffs.

"Yes I am!" replies the shy deer with a loud snort. "What has happened to my lovely little Dottie? Will she be all right?" she continues, nervous and frightened for her young fawn.

Bear and Katie realize they recognize the beautiful deer standing by the edge of the woods.

"Why, I believe it's Duchess!" barks Bear.

"Is that you, Duchess?" cries Katie.

"Why, is that you, Bear and Katie?"

Bear and Katie and Duchess are happy to see each other again. It was back in the spring of the year when they met at Prices' Maple Farm.*

---

*See, *Bear & Katie in A Day with Friends*

Meanwhile, Dad and the sleigh driver tug and pull. "I'll count to three and we'll both lift at the same time," says the driver.

"I agree," answers Dad. "Just tell me when."

The driver looks around. "Bear and Katie! Step aside! We're going to get Dottie free from this tree once and for all," he tells them. "Okay, here we go! One—two—three—now lift!" the driver says.

Both men lift with all their strength, tugging, pulling and grunting with all their might. Their faces turn red, showing the strain from the weight of the huge tree branch.

"Dottie is free!" shout the two black labs as their barks of happiness are heard all the way back to where the sleigh is parked on the trail.

Dad and the sleigh driver are happy that they are finally able to release Dottie from under the giant tree branch.

Bear and Katie are relieved. "We sure are glad you are free from that awful tree branch," Katie tells the little fawn, with a happy bark.

"Me, too!" says Bear.

"No one can be happier than me," whimpers Dottie. "But my leg sure hurts," she continues.

"Now we must get your leg bandaged," Dad tells Dottie.

"Not until she sees her mother!" shouts the pretty deer standing by the edge of the woods. She makes her way over to take a look at her beautiful fawn. Then she rubs her nose against Dottie's nose, giving her a big deer kiss. "How are you, my lovely little fawn? I have been so worried about you. You shouldn't go running off on your own yet. You're still a bit too young for that, you know."

"I'm sorry I worried you," cries Dottie with a soft snort. "I won't be doing that again, I promise. But... lucky for me," she continues, with a nervous sound in her voice, "I'm lucky I had Bear and Katie here to rescue me." She looks at her mother with a big painful grin on her little spotted face, then looks up at her rescuers, her heroes.

Bear and Katie are so delighted to see that Dottie and her mother, Duchess, are together again.

"Thank you, Bear and Katie, for saving my little Dottie," snorts Duchess.

"Oh, it was nothing," bark the two dogs. "We are happy we were here to help."
"I hope we will see you again," says the little fawn.

"Oh, you can bet on it!" answers Katie. "We come here every year, and to Prices' Maple Farm, too," she laughs, turning around, doing a little Katie twist.

"Well then!" say Duchess and Dottie, at the same time, "we'll see you girls somewhere soon. Somewhere on down the road," they laugh.

"And I won't be getting under any fallen tree branches," chuckles Dottie, holding her painful leg slightly off the ground, walking with a limp.

"Oh! By the way Katie, you and Dottie need to be more careful when you wander off into the woods alone," says Duchess with a big deer grin.

Katie looks surprised. She is thinking about the boulder incident. "Could it have been Duchess that bumped me and knocked me out of the way of the falling boulder?"

Katie gives Duchess a nod and woofs. "So... it was you who pushed me out of the way of that giant boulder?" she asks her.

"Why... yes it was!" snorts the beautiful deer. "And I'm glad that I did. Look at what a wonderful thing you did, Bear and Katie. You rescued my precious Dottie."

Bear, Katie, Dad and the driver look at one another and smile.

The sleigh driver calls back to his office and asks for help. "We have a hurt fawn that needs assistance right away," he says. "Send someone as quick as you can."

"You and Dottie stay right here. Help is on the way," Dad tells Duchess.

"We'll be right here. Thank you," says the lovely deer. "Thank you for your help. All of you that is," she says, as she looks around at her friends Bear and Katie.

"Well! Now, let's get back to the sleigh ride, shall we?" says the driver, with a very happy sound in his rough voice.

Bear and Katie head back to the sleigh. Everyone is happy to see the heroes of the day return to finish their ride. They all begin to cheer.

Dad is happy to help his two heroes onto the sleigh.

Suddenly everyone begins to sing. "Dashing through the snow, in a one horse open sleigh...," a song appropriate for the occasion.

Bear and Katie raise their heads and howl their own tune, as they enjoy the snowflakes falling on their noses.

The sleigh driver is so pleased about Bear and Katie rescuing the small fawn and that the heroes of the day are riding with him, that he takes them on an extra long trip through the woods.

Bear and Katie truly enjoyed the sleigh ride.

"Well girls, I believe it's time we head back to the house," says Dad.

Finding the Perfect Tree

"We still have to get a Christmas tree!" shout Bear and Katie.

"Oh yes!" answers Dad, "we will have to find a tree farm on the way home. We want to pick out a beautiful tree before it gets dark," Dad continues. "After all, it's Christmas Eve, and you know who comes on Christmas Eve!" he tells them.

Bear and Katie race each other to the truck. They take their places, happy to settle in for the long trip home. But Bear and Katie aren't settled in for long before Mom spots a tree farm.

"There's a tree farm! What do you think, should we stop?" she says anxiously. "It looks like a nice place to look for the perfect tree."

"Oh! Yes," barks Bear. "Katie and I are good at finding the perfect tree."

"Let's stop!" Katie ruffs.

Dad turns into the entrance of the farm, and drives right up to the edge of the trees. He opens the door and both dogs leap out, and then look to Dad for a signal to go.

"Okay girls, let's find a nice tree," he tells them.

Mom and Dad head in one direction. Bear and Katie head in the other, sniffing at each and every tree. Bear looks up and down for the perfect height. Katie looks back and forth for the perfect width. They are sure they are going to find the perfect tree.

After looking at more than a dozen trees, Bear stops short. "Here it is, Katie! What do you think? I just love it!" Bear continues with a bark. "Check out the width."

Katie steps aside and takes a long look. "Why... I think you're right, Bear. It's just beautiful! It looks better than all the others we have been looking at."

"Let's bark for Mom and Dad," Bear tells Katie.

The two of them sit by the tree they believe is the perfect one. Both of them let out three loud barks.

In an instant, Mom and Dad appear. "Well... what have you girls found?" says Dad, rubbing Bear on the head with one hand and rubbing Katie's head with the other.

"We believe we found just the right tree," ruffs Bear.

"Well now, let's take a look," says Dad. "You know how fussy mom can be," he continues.

Dad looks at mom. "Well... what do you think about this tree?" he asks with a smile. Bear and Katie wagging their tails, are excited as they watch Mom's expression. They are anxious to see if she likes the tree.

Mom walks around and around the tree to examine it.

She looks at her two happy dogs. She gives them a big grin, then looks at Dad. "I do believe this is the perfect tree," she tells him.

Bear and Katie jump for joy. They take a few rolls in the snow and then shake themselves off.

Dad heads for the truck to get the saw, and returns to the tree.

After cutting down the tree, the farmer puts it on a machine he has that wraps the tree and ties it down for the long trip home.

Bear and Katie are anxious to get the tree into the house. Mom rushes to find the ornaments and Dad rushes to find the lights. Bear and Katie help to put the tree in the tree stand, holding it straight, so Dad can tighten it at the bottom.

Mom brings a big bowl of popcorn into the room along with the ornaments. They all work together to decorate their beautiful tree.

Bear and Katie look for their favorite decorations, Christmas bulbs with their pictures on them. The two labs are having the time of their life, nibbling on popcorn, watching Mom and Dad decorate the tree they picked out.

Bear helps Dad by holding the bulbs one at a time with her mouth, while Katie makes a mess as she helps herself to a bowl of popcorn.

Dad places the final decoration on the top of the tree, a large star.

Mom comes in with an armful of gifts to place under the tree.

Dad does the honors of turning on the lights.

"It's just beautiful," ruffs Bear.

"It's the prettiest tree in all of New England," ruffs Katie.

"This is the perfect Christmas," says Bear. "With the snow falling and the ride on a sleigh... the whole day has been wonderful."

"Sure makes a dog... happy to be a dog," laughs Katie, making her way back to the bowl of popcorn Mom set aside for her precious dogs.

Bear and Katie nibble on more popcorn and then rush off to bed. They know tomorrow will be Christmas Day.

Katie begins to talk about their adventure during the sleigh ride and Bear tells Katie how happy she was to rescue Duchess's small fawn Dottie. They wonder where the two deer are on this quiet Christmas night.

They laugh about Katie falling into the skaters, and how much fun they had building snowmen with the children, especially the snow-dogs that looked just like them.

As the two dogs drift off to sleep, Duchess and her fawn Dottie peer through the window. Bear dreams of getting a new Frisbee and a big chewy, while Katie dreams of getting new tennis balls, her favorite ball to retrieve. Duchess and Dottie look at each other and smile.

The two labs have had a long exciting day and certainly this will be their very special Christmas to remember.

The End

About Bear

Bear is gentle, caring, very intelligent and quick thinking. She always obeys the rules and loves playing the role of Katie's protector. Her hobbies include riding around with Dad, retrieving balls and chasing squirrels. Bear welcomes a pat on the head from everyone she meets. Bear, a female black lab/shepherd mix, wandered her way to our doorstep when she was only six weeks old. Bear always wears a collar.

About Katie

Katie is fun loving, a bit too friendly, and is always getting into trouble. She loves her best friend Bear and knows Bear will always come to her rescue. Katie finds trouble everywhere she goes. Her hobbies are swimming, retrieving balls and frisbee. She was rescued at the last minute from a dog pound when she was six months old. Katie is a female black lab. Katie prefers to wear a scarf.

About the Author

Loni R. Burchette was born in
Ashland, Kentucky. It was only
when she moved to New
Hampshire that she finally

found a place she could love as much as the
beautiful "Blue Grass State" she hails from.
Along with her husband and four of her five
children, she now makes the Lakes Region of
New Hampshire her home. Her hobbies are
writing, art and traveling.

About the Illustrator

Patricia Sweet-MacDonald was
born in Clearwater, Florida.
She moved to New Hampshire
in 2002, with her husband,

Michael and two children, Alison and Brendan.
She started painting at age 5 and has never quit.

More About Amherst (Ammy) 1993 – 2004

Ammy was a showy Boxer born in Sudbury, Massachusetts at the Belcore Kennels. Mother: Lady Lover. Father: Jack.

Ammy was a loving companion and best friend to her owners. She had a wonderful personality, loved to sing, enjoyed family gatherings and loved getting in the middle of a conversation. Ammy's favorite pastime was lying on the floor on her side while letting anyone rub her tummy with their foot. She is sadly missed by her family and will always have a place in their hearts. "Amherst is at peace guarding our comings and goings," her owners tell us.

Future Bear and Katie Books

A Day With Friends

A Riverboat Ride on the Ohio

A Day at the Beach and Katie Gets Arrested

Bear and Katie at the Kentucky Derby
   "Run for the Roses"

Lost in the White Mountains

Bear and Katie See the Big Apple

In the Badlands with Mr. Wanbli (Eagle)

A Day with Mato the Bear

Visit our website at www.bearandkatie.com